MW01070501

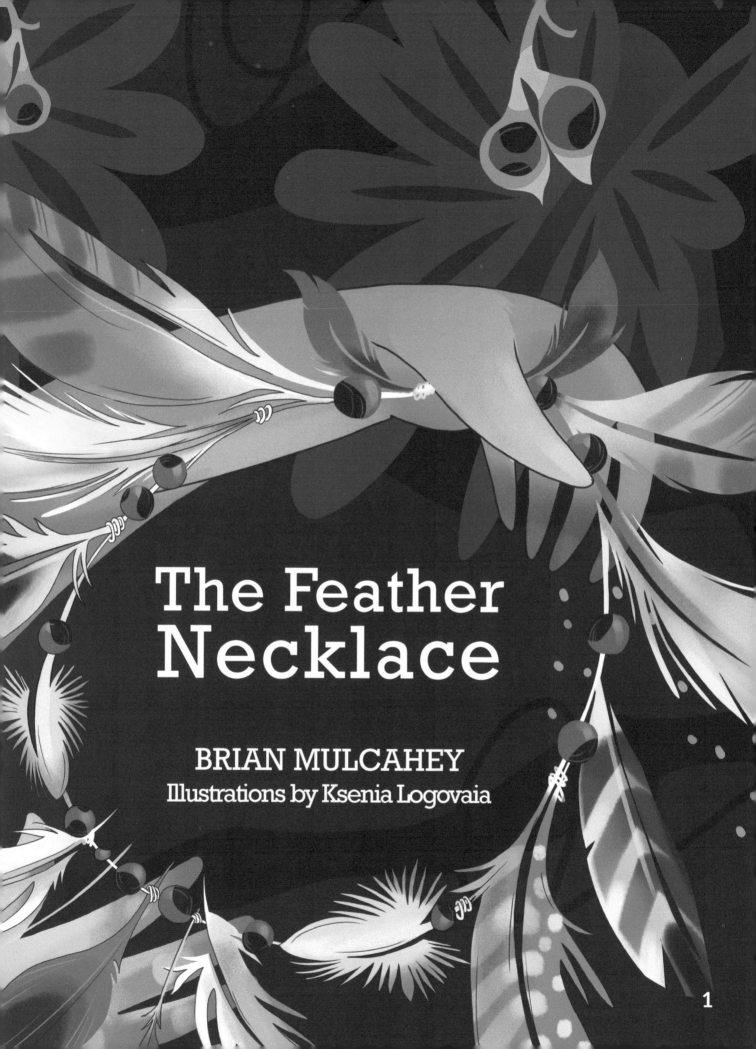

The Feather Necklace

BRIAN MULCAHEY

Illustrations by Ksenia Logovaia

The Feather Necklace
Copyright © 2023 by Brian Mulcahey

All rights reserved. No part of this publication may be reproduced, distributed, or transmitted in any form or by any means, including photocopying, recording or other electronic or mechanical methods, without the prior written permission of the author, except in the case of brief quotations embodied in reviews and certain other non-commercial uses permitted by copyright law.

Printed in the United States of America

Hardcover ISBN: 978-1-959096-89-4
Paperback ISBN: 978-1-959096-90-0
Ebook ISBN: 978-1-959096-91-7
Library of Congress Control Number: 2023939969

DartFrog Plus
A division of DartFrog Books
4697 Main Street
Manchester Center, VT 05255

To Eliza, my little explorer.

And to my Kukama and Peruvian scientist friends who helped inspire this story.

This work could not have been completed without the unrelenting support of my wife, Nicole. Thank you to Sirah Jarocki for helping edit early versions of this book, and to Kimberlyn Chota Pinedo for giving me the courage to share the book with the world. Thanks and gratitude also go to Rosa Vallejos Yopán and Rosa Amias Murayari for their publication Diccionario Kukama-Kukamiria * Castellano. I relied heavily on this work for translating words into the Kukama language.

In the jungles of Peru, three young scientists docked their canoe on a riverbank. The river's water had been stained a sweet black color by the fallen leaves, just like a cup of tea.

The forest in front of them was so dense it looked like a green castle wall. There were no paths or roads. No human sounds besides their own voices.

"I'm heading east to look for monkeys. Let's meet back here at sunset. The one with the best discovery of the day wins!" the first scientist said playfully.

He grabbed his things from the canoe, which included a camera, a compass, a raincoat, binoculars, some data sheets, and a GPS.

"I'm heading west to look for butterflies!" said the second scientist who carried her butterfly net, a satellite phone, special pink tape to mark the trees as she went, and some rotten bananas for the insects.

The third scientist, well that was me, Tulio. I am from the Kukama tribe and this forest is my backyard.

I didn't need much gear for the day: just my boots, pitachirus, a machete, kichi, and the skills I had learned as a boy.

"My people taught me how to navigate through the jungle without getting lost. See you at sunset," I told my friends with a wink.

As I walked through the jungle, I moved rhythmically like a dancer, chopping a path with my machete.

Whap, womp, whoosh went the leaves and branches as I cut the trail. I scanned for animal tracks while avoiding spiny plants, singing as I went. "Buenas noches, dulces sueños. Te amo, te amo, mi corazón."
Goodnight, sweet dreams.
I love you, I love you, my heart.

13

The jungle was getting thicker. As the hours went by, I grew tired. Where was the best discovery of the day?

Suddenly, I heard the jungle come to life. Hooting and squawking. Roaring and whistling. I'd heard these noises before, but never all at once!

Keeping very quiet,
I climbed up a kapok
tree and was surprised
to see so many animals
together in one place.

16

The jaguar, aimanta, was there. The anaconda, iwirati tsukuri, too. The tapir, tapira, and the howler monkeys, akiki. They all seemed to be watching something. But what were they looking at?

"El desfile de moda de aves!" I whispered.
A bird fashion show! My grandfather
told me stories about them, but those
were just bedtime stories, weren't they?

I climbed even higher for a better look. All the most beautiful jungle birds had come together.

The black-collared
hawk and the snail
kite, wayari and
wiratsu mama,
mirrored each
other in flight.

The umbrella birds,
yakupena, strutted
and spun while the
hummingbirds,
mainuma, buzzed
in great circles.

The scythebill, iti, and the
aracari, aratsari, hopped
side by side, flashing
their beautiful beaks.

22

The woodpecker, chunaki, and motmot, yiriwa, kicked and crushed branches to show off their strength.

The cacique,
yapu, and masked
tanager, tsiin,
started to bob,
weave, and wiggle.

24

"Oh wow!"
I blurted in astonishment.
But I was too loud.
The animals on the ground
scattered in every direction.
All the birds launched
into the air.

By the time I came
down the tree,
I was all alone.

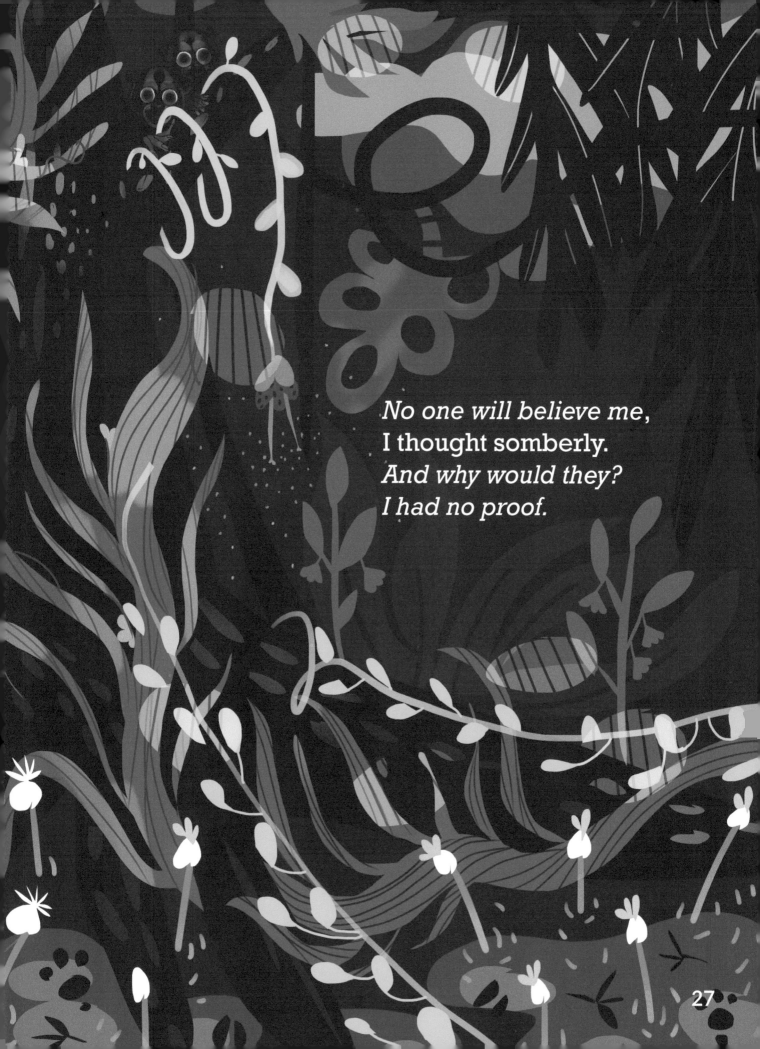

No one *will* believe me,
I thought somberly.
And why would they?
I had no proof.

I closed my eyes and began to sing again, trying to lift my spirits. "Buenas noches, dulces sueños, te amo, te amo, mi corazón."

28

But the birds had not flown far away. As I sang, feathers floated down to the forest floor.

"The birds must have enjoyed my song!" I chuckled softly. I collected a feather from each bird at the show.

As I retraced my steps
to the river, I delicately
strung the feathers and
some nearby seeds into
a necklace, a yachukarin.
When I showed my friends
at the canoe a few hours
later, they were amazed.

"You saw all these birds at once?" The monkey scientist exclaimed in disbelief as he looked closer at each feather. "I've only seen half these species in my whole life!"

"You win the competition, Tulio," said the butterfly scientist. "My only prize was losing a boot in the mud. Your prize is being our leader on the next trip."

33

I smiled. "I've never seen anything like that bird show before. I feel grateful. I might never see it again. But maybe we'll find it again together."

As we pushed the canoe off the bank, I placed the necklace over my head and against my heart, my iya. I was proud to be Kukama.

An ipirawira pitana, a baby river dolphin, broke the stillness with a breath. Its mother rose right beside it with a nuzzle. Giant river otters, yawarpana, crunched catfish for dinner. The light of sunset shimmered off the water surface, turning the water from black to gold.

About the Kukama

The Kukama (Cocama, Kokama, or Kukama-Kukamiria) people live in the Loreto Region of the Peruvian Amazon. With an ethnic population of approximately 20,000, they preserve vast knowledge about the forest and the aquatic environment. By collaborating with international and Peruvian scientists, such as those from the non-profit FundAmazonia, the Kukama have developed, implemented, and refined increasingly sustainable wildlife conservation practices, particularly in the Tamshiyacu-Tahuayo Community Reserve and the Pacaya-Samiria National Reserve. However, global climate change will continue to cause disruptions to their ways of life.

The Kukama language is also considered highly endangered. There are only around 1000 fluent speakers left. Although Spanish is the language taught in schools, organizations like the Formación de Maestros Bilingües de la Amazonía (FORMABIAP) have begun to rebalance curricula to include both western and local input. Teaching Kukama as a second language has begun in many village schools.

Kukama Glossary (In order of appearance)

Boots- Pitachirus
Machete- Kichi
Jaguar (*Panthera onca*)- Aimanta
Green anaconda (*Eunectes murinus*)- Iwirati Tsukuri
South American Tapir (*Tapirus terrestris*)- Tapira
Red-Howler Monkey (*Alouatta seniculus*)- Akiki
Black-collared Hawk (*Busarellus nigricollis*)- Wayari
Snail Kite (*Rostrhamus sociabilis*)- Wiratsu Mama
Umbrella Bird (*Cephalopterus ornatus*)- Yakupena
Hummingbird- Mainuma
      Festive Coquette (*Lophornis chalybeus*)
      Long-tailed Hermit (*Phaethornis superciliosus*)
      Fiery Topaz (*Topaza pyra*)
      Marvelous Spatuletail (*Loddigesia mirabilis*)
Curve-billed Scythebill (*Campylorhamphus procurvoides*)- Iti
Chestnut-eared Aracari (*Pteroglossus castanotis*) - Aratsari
Cream-colored Woodpecker (*Celeus flavus*)- Chunaki
Amazonian Motmot (*Motmotus momota*)- Yiriwa
Yellow-rumped Cacique (*Cacicus solitarius*)- Yapu
Masked Tanager (*Stilpnia nigrocinta*)- Tsiin
Necklace- Yachukarin
Heart-Iya
Pink River Dolphin (*Inia geoffrensis*)- Ipirawira Pitana
Giant River Otter (*Pteronura brasiliensis*)- Yawarpana

Other wildlife:

Insects-

      Amber Phantom (*Haetera piera*)

      Menalaus Blue Morpho (*Morpho menelaus*)

      Giant Owl (*Caligo eurilochus*)

      Leaf Cutter Ants (*Atta cephalotes*)

Mammals-

      Three-toed Sloth (*Bradypus variegatus*)

      Peruvian Night Monkey (*Aotus miconax*)

Birds-

      Horned Screamer (*Anhima cornuta*)

      Harpy Eagle (*Harpia harpyja*)

      Andean Cock-of-the-rock (*Rupicola peruvianu*)

      Cocoi Heron (*Ardea cocoi*)

      Green Honeycreeper (*Chlorophanes Spiza*)

      Red-and-green Macaw (*Ara chloropterus*)

      Blue-and-yellow Macaw (*Ara arauna*)

      Silver-beaked Tanager (*Rhampocelus carbo*)

      Amazon Kingfisher (*Chlorocerly amazona*)

Brian Mulcahey has been an educator and scientist for the last decade. He received his Bachelors in Zoology and Mandarin from the University of Vermont and a Masters in Teaching Biological Science from Miami University. In 2023, he received the National Science Teacher Association's Yager Award for Excellence in Teaching. His extensive field experience includes studying birds of the South Pacific, the Yucatan Peninsula, and the Peruvian Amazon.

Brian believes that one of the best ways to support wildlife conservation is by shining the light on the knowledge and effort by indigenous scientists and communities.

About the Illustrator

Ksenia Logovaia is a Belarusian artist and illustrator, a mom and traveller, a dog and horse lover! She comes from Minsk, Belarus and now lives in Poland. She adores drawing and painting while traveling—her sketchbook is always with her. She illustrated *The Feather Necklace* during a cold, Nordic winter, taking in the spirit of tropical heat and colors.

Printed in the USA
CPSIA information can be obtained
at www.ICGtesting.com
LVHW070024310823
756749LV00013B/43